Re

Recollections

Edna Mary Wood

Paper Doll

©Edna Mary Wood

Published 1998 by Paper Doll
Belasis Hall
Coxwold Way
Billingham
Cleveland

ISBN: 1 86248 999 8

Printed by Lintons Printers, Co. Durham

*For Ted, June, Vicki
and friends*

CONTENTS

God Where Are You?	1
Why?	2
Angel Friend	3
No Passport Needed	4
Manners	5
Early Summer	6
Autumn	7
An Old Church Yard	8
Dreams	9
Starry Skies	10
Spring	11
Lottery	12
Rain	13
Early Morn'	14
Waiting	15
The Fair	16
Hope	17
A Friend	18
Birds	19
The Garden	20
The Club	21
Luck?	22
My Dog	23
Imagination	24
Ups and Downs	25
Prayer	26
Clouds	27
Memories	28
Morning Mist	29
The Earth	30

GOD WHERE ARE YOU ?

In the night I lie awake
And pray for day to break,
At last I see dawn's hue -
God where are you?

I hear birds sing,
Feel the wind,
See the view,
Beauty all around -
God where are you found?

I've seen clouds from above and below,
Heard language I do not know,
Friendly smiles here and o'er sea -
God where can you be?

I've been deaf and blind,
No matter where I've looked,
You I could not find.
But you've been with me night and day
Oh God, thank you I pray.

WHY ?

Why can't you hear a noise
When clouds bump together,
You can see them meet,
Mix and change shape,
But not a sound, not a squeak.

When a leaf falls from a tree,
Why can't you hear it hit the ground,
You can see it flutter on its way,
But hear not a sound.

A snow flake drifts to earth,
Falls on trees, hills, all over the place,
You can see it's beauty everywhere,
But not a sound can be heard.

ANGEL FRIEND

I have a special friend,
God loaned her to me,
She does her best to keep me from harm,
Without any help on my part.
Tries to keep me doing right,
Both by day and night,
But I don't always listen
To her advice.
Just go my own way
'I'm sorry', to her I say.
There's lots I'd like to do
But life is passing by.
When my last days are through
It will be too late,
I'll be sorry then,
My guardian Angel friend
For not listening to you.

NO PASSPORT NEEDED

No passport needed,
No fences or stiles to climb,
No forms to fill in,
No visa to find.
Just the belief
God's face we shall see.

No barrier or frontier,
Wealth is not needed,
No need to beg,
No more money - all will be fed.
For God has promised
All will be welcome.

No colour bar,
Religious or special race,
All will be equal.
So in prayers praise His name,
Shout it out loud - don't hide your face,
Enter God's kingdom
In favour and grace.

MANNERS

"Please", it's not hard to say
For things you may want,
Or have done.
And "Thank You" -
Such simple words,
Can mean so much to someone,
For something passed,
A kindness done,
For help in some way.
"Sorry", is it so hard to say,
For a harsh word
Or an unkind remark?
A smile can help cheer
Someone feeling low,
A lonely person.
Such simple things -
So try them out,
And make someone's day!

EARLY SUMMER

Beneath the canopy of green,
Wild life moves around unseen,
Songs of birds fill the air,
Leaves rustle in the breeze,
While here and there,
Sunbeams shine through the trees,
Out from the cool dimness of the wood,
Into full sunshine and warm air.
The coo-coo of pigeons and doves
In the trees up above,
Pink and white wild roses
And honeysuckle scent in the air.
A few fluffy clouds drift lazily by
In the bright blue sky.

AUTUMN

Old leaves rustle on the ground
As the cool breeze
Blows softly in the trees.
For Autumn has arrived,
With reds, bronze, golds and greens,
As leaves start to fall all around.

On Brambles, blackberries ripen,
And bunches of scarlet berries
On Rowan trees lie.
But soon all will be bare
And the colours will fade away,
As Nature's treasures all decay.

AN OLD CHURCH YARD

I remember an old church yard
That had lain unused and neglected,
Had been for many years.
For no one went there any more,
The graves were over grown,
Angels, crosses and head stones
Covered with moss, ivy or lichen,
Some leaning or broken,
Words faded or lost from sight.
But wild life was always there,
Flowers, though wild, bloomed
Most of the year.
In the many trees,
Birds sang like a choir,
While the dead lay in peace,
All safe in that tranquil,
Peaceful place of their own Eden.

DREAMS

Any one can have a dream, a wish
Of a bungalow in the country,
A safe haven from all cares,
Garden of peace and beauty.

Of a cottage by the sea,
To hear the seagulls cry,
Waves that murmur on the shore,
To stroll along a lonely beach.

Of a car that you can drive
Along lonely roads,
So fresh and care free,
Feel good to be alive.

Of a caravan in a beauty spot,
You can take anywhere,
Country, sea or lakes.
So remember to have a dream,
Or a wish to come true,
It's always up to you.

STARRY SKIES

When I was a little girl,
In the streets there was soft gas light,
The stars were a joy to see,
For millions filled the night time skies,
Even seen in bright moonlight.

When I was a young woman,
There was a war,
The night had a different hue,
As fires and dust filled the air,
A bomber's moon still sailed on,
The starry sky was still there.

Now I'm old the night sky,
Shines with electric lights.,
The moon still sails on,
And though the stars are still there,
Only few can be seen,
For now they are hidden from our sight,
In that polluted night sky.

SPRING

The air is fresh in the morning sun,
Skylark rises high,
His song fills the air.
Gorse and broom,
Dandelions and butter cups
With gold gleams,
Purple clover, daisies white,
Surrounded by a sea of green.
On the branches of the fir trees,
Like candles new growth shows,
Butterflies dance lazily by,
Bees hum, birds sing,
It's so good to be alive
On this God's good Earth.

LOTTERY

Saturday night, lottery time,
All the glitter of the show,
Some star sings,
People cheer and clap,
Then comes the compere,
Says what's in the kitty,
That someone can win,
Drops the number balls
Into the rolling bin,
A voice calls out a number,
Eight, thirty-three and five,
My heart races I've got them,
My hopes then fade,
For the others are not mine -
But I'm happy I've won a tenner.

RAIN

Rain beats down on the window,
The drops run down the panes
In their own little races;
Clouds scuttle across the skies.
As the rain stops,
Drops still fall from the trees,
All looks clean,
Washed from above.
Flowers raise their heads
As the sun shines once again.
Birds shake their feathers
And sing their songs -
It's a wonderful world to be in.

EARLY MORN'

After the night rain
The early morning sun shines,
Lights up rain drops on the grass and leaves,
They shine like millions of diamonds
That have been scattered around
With colours of different hues.
The air is fresh,
Scent of broom fills the air,
As you look past the trees,
Over meadows of green
And ploughed ground
To the forests of the Ercall and Wrekin.
And the TV mast way up above,
Points to the sky
Like a finger way up high.

WAITING

In the Doctor's waiting room,
The sun shone through the windows,
Each person having a look,
At each new arrival.
Some smile, some cough,
Glance at a watch,
How much longer? -
Time goes by...
A name called,
Goes to the appointed room.
At last it's me,
A sigh of relief
As in I go to voice my woe.

THE FAIR

Red, green and white stripes
Of the covered stalls,
Loud music calling people
To the fair.
Bright lights, prizes galore,
Roll up, roll up, win a prize,
Try your luck,
Go on sir, knock off a coconut!
Painted horses gallop round,
Laughter fills the air,
Swings ride high,
Helter skelter and big dipper,
Squeals and shouts and candy floss,
As we all enjoy
The fun of the fairground.

HOPE

The phone rings,
Who can it be?
Hope it's not a wrong number,
But someone to talk to me.

Life can be lonely at times.

Post man comes,
What can it be?
Not a circular, I hope,
But a nice letter for me.

There's a knock at the door,
Now who is that?
Not someone selling -
No it's my friend, come for a chat.

A FRIEND

An old friend of mine died today,
She made me feel good,
Always made clouds fade away,
As on our way we would run.
Temperamental at times, she was,
Grumbling at some hills,
Always glad on the flat.
I've known her since her prime,
But now her time is passed -
That grand old banger of mine.

BIRDS

The Blackbird in the tree,
Sang his song,
Is it just for me?
I sprinkle crumbs,
Fill the bird bath,
Put out some seeds
On the bird table.
Watch from my window,
See them bathe,
Spray the water all around,
It looks like rain drops
When it hits the ground.

THE GARDEN

Mow the grass,
Weed the garden,
Sweep up some leaves off the path.
In my dreams;
For the grass is too wet to mow,
Weeds have taken over,
Leaves fall faster
Than I can sweep,
Winter comes too fast,
But maybe next Spring
I will catch up at last.

THE CLUB

At the club
We have a laugh,
A good gossip,
Always glad to meet
Old and new friends.
Just once a week,
But it's great,
For it gets you out.
Though we are all old,
We are young at heart,
At Age Concern,
Still glad to be a part.

LUCK ?

Get up late,
Everything goes wrong,
No matter how I try.
Burn the toast,
Knock over my drink,
The car won't start,
So call a cab;
But that is late.
At last I'm there,
But it's the wrong time,
And I had forgot
They had altered the clock....
Just not my day!

MY DOG

In the homeless dog kennels,
I first saw him being walked,
Rough sandy coat, brown eyes,
Tail curled over his back.
Four years old,
Leo is his name.
He licks my hand,
Wags his tail,
I see the trust in his eyes.
Get his lead,
No matter what the weather,
As on our walks we go.
He runs on to follow trails,
Ears alert, eyes bright,
Wag of his tail.
Then back to the home
I know he is glad to see.

IMAGINATION

I thought I heard the sea,
But it was only the breeze
Blowing through the trees.
The leaves, they rustled
Like shingle on the shore.

I heard the gulls call,
Just like at the beach,
But it was land gulls
On the ploughed fields I heard.

I see the sun shine and glint
On tower block windows,
They look like waves
Dancing on the sea.
Imagination can paint
Many pictures in the mind,
That can seem so real to me.

UPS AND DOWNS

A lift goes up,
A lift comes down.
Life's like that,
Gives you a smile,
Gives you a frown.
Climb the stairs,
Go down again,
What's in the middle
To share your cares -
Best to find out,
To have a friend,
Someone to share
Your laughter and tears.
Then comes the day
You only go up,
Hope not to come down.

PRAYER

Jesus taught the people
The Lord's prayer.
Just think of how many,
In many languages,
Have said that prayer.
We still say it today,
As our ancestors did.
How many other words,
Through the years,
Have lasted so long,
Have been passed down,
That will always mean so much,
To help us in our lives,
And will go on always,
For ever more.

CLOUDS

Darkness of the night,
Faded from sight.
The sun rose in a cloudy sky,
That turned the clouds
To a red glow,
That gradually went to gold.
As the dawn grew brighter,
Silver edged to white they went,
From white to grey did go.
As the morning passed by,
Darker went the clouds,
Then the rain
Fell to the earth below.

MEMORIES

A path of memories,
Follow you through life.
They start the day
That you can think.
It's up to each
To store the best we can;
Smiles and love from our mothers,
Advice from our Dad,
Happiness through life,
Friends we have.
Day we got married,
Love of a partner,
Children we had,
All memories that last
'Til the day we depart
From this earthly life.

MORNING MIST

The morning mist rolled across
Fields like a grey blanket,
Enveloped all it touched.
As it grew nearer
It's cool, damp fingers
Curled all around
In nooks and corners,
Not rising very high,
About two or three feet off the ground.
Gave an eerie feeling.
'Til the early morning sun,
Slowly burned it all away,
To another bright day.

THE EARTH

God made the Earth,
And gave it to man
For his safe keeping.
But since then
We have had wars, revolutions,
Cut and burned the forests,
Polluted the seas and rivers,
Ruined the land in all ways.
Then we ask God why
He let these things happen?
But it's not him,
It is us who do all these things
To this wonderful world of ours.